THE CACTUS BOYS

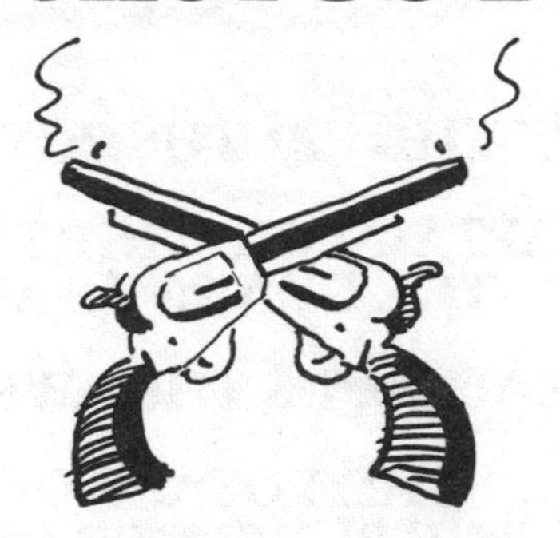

THE CACTUS BOYS

CAPTAIN MIDNIGHT AND
THE GRANNY BAG

GALACTACUS THE AWESOME

THE VOYAGE OF
THE PURPLE PRAWN

THE CACTUS BOYS

Andrew Matthews

Illustrated by
André Amstutz

ORCHARD BOOKS

for Sarah and William
A.M.

ORCHARD BOOKS
96 Leonard Street, London EC2A 4RH
Orchard Books Australia
14 Mars Road, Lane Cove, NSW 2066
ISBN 1 85213 779 7 Hardback
ISBN 1 85213 876 9 Paperback
First published in Great Britain 1994

A CIP catalogue record for this book is available
from the British Library.
Printed in Great Britain.

CONTENTS

WANTED!

DEAD OR ALIVE

BILLY THE KID

JESSE JAMES

THE CACTUS BOYS

1
FAMOUS OUTLAWS

THERE were many famous outlaws in the old Wild West. Billy the Kid and Jesse James were tough, mean and quick on the draw. But of all the famous outlaws, none was tougher or meaner than the members of the gang known as the Cactus Boys.

There were three of them. The leader was Red Dog Holliday. He was a big man with a stubbly chin and a laugh that sounded like a hound-dog with a horse standing on its paw. He could draw his gun in the blink of an eye and his aim was deadly.

Snake-Eyes Masterson spoke in a hissing voice and had a thin moustache that looked like a piece of black spaghetti stuck to his top lip. His draw was speedier than a striking rattler and he was so mean that daisies closed their petals when his shadow fell on them.

The third member of the gang was Dude Kincaid. He wore a black hat with a silver band, a dark suit with a frilly white shirt and a fancy waistcoat. Dude's draw was so fast that he had to slow it down so that people could see it. Dude smiled a lot, but behind the smile was a heart that was colder than a penguin's flipper.

The Cactus Boys' hide-out was an old shack on the edge of the Pecos Desert, where no posse would ever think of looking. It had been ages since the gang's last low-down act and the men were bored.

Snake-Eyes had stuck his Bowie knife into the door so many times that the wood had more holes in it than a doughnut factory. Dude was playing patience, and cheating. Red Dog was on a chair in the corner looking at a map that was so greasy, his fingers squeaked when they touched it.

Suddenly Red Dog stamped his foot, sending hundreds of cockroaches scuttling for cover.

"Jumpin' Jehosophat!" he roared. "I reckon as how we got a price on our heads in every consarned state in the country! We must've robbed every bank, train and stage between here and the Rio Grande!"

"So what?" hissed Snake-Eyes.

"Maybe it's time to think of movin' on," said Red Dog.

"Where?" asked Snake Eyes.

"Canada," said Red Dog.

"Brr! Too cold!" grumbled Snake-Eyes.

"Mexico, then," Red Dog suggested.

"No way!" shuddered Snake-Eyes. "They got them big, hairy tarantulas down in Mexico!"

"Well, what d'you think, Dude?" asked Red Dog.

"I think that if I catch myself cheatin' one more time, I'm gonna drag me outside and have a gunfight with myself!" said Dude.

Red Dog jabbed at the map with a stubby finger. "Can't go to Denver, we robbed a bank there last spring. Can't go to Tombstone because we held up a stage there in the fall. Where in tarnation can we go? I'm a rootin', tootin' outlaw who's plumb run out of places to root and toot!"

"Why don't we go back to Dodge City?" suggested Snake-Eyes.

"Because we've robbed every bank there," said Red Dog. "Plus every saloon and hardware store. We've rustled cattle and sheep from Dodge – why, we've even rustled chickens! We've robbed Dodge City so many times that there ain't any-thin' left there worth takin'!"

“How about here?” said Dude, pointing to a dot on the map.

“Aw, that’s just a baked-bean stain,” Red Dog told him.

“No it ain’t!” said Dude. “There’s writin’ on it!” He drew his gun with lightning speed and fired four shots at a filthy window. The glass shattered and sunlight flooded the shack. Dude held the map up to the light and peered closely at it.

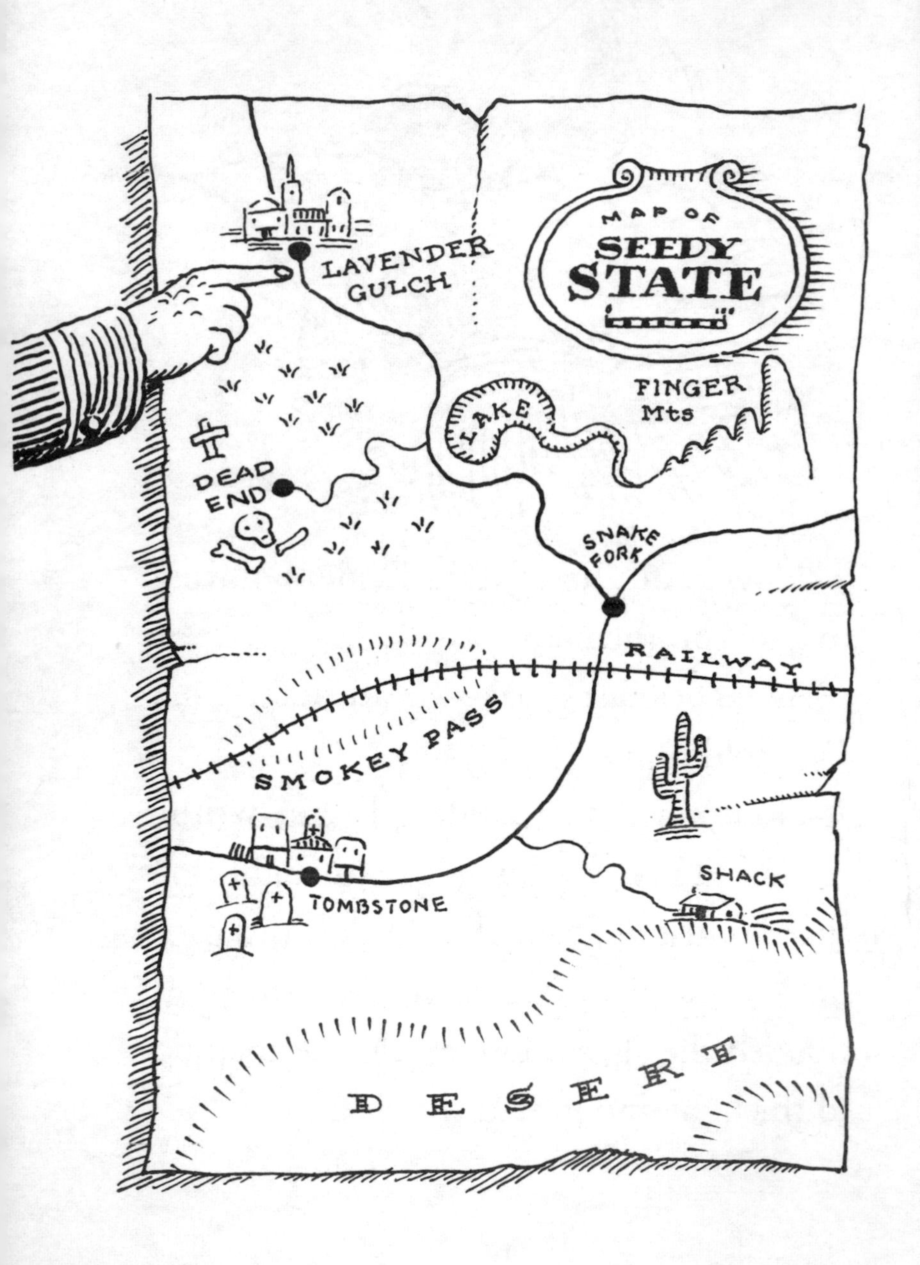
MAP OF
SEEDY
STATE
LAVENDER
GULCH
LAKE
FINGER
Mts
DEAD
END
SNAKE
FORK
RAILWAY
SMOKEY PASS
TOMBSTONE
SHACK
DESERT

"Lavender Gulch," he read aloud.

"Lavender Gulch?" said Snake Eyes. "I ain't never heard of it."

"Me neither," said Red Dog.

Dude looked at them and smiled a smile as thin as the edge of a razor. "Well," he said, "if we ain't heard of Lavender Gulch, maybe Lavender Gulch ain't heard of us...Haw, haw!"

"Yeah!" exclaimed Snake-Eyes. "Haw, haw!"

Red Dog knocked off Snake-Eyes' hat. "Don't you go 'haw, haw' before me, Snake-Eyes!" Red Dog growled. "I'm the big boss-man of this gang and don't you forget it! Now, I reckon we ought to get ourselves some shut-eye, because tomorrow we're gonna take a little trip down to Lavender Gulch!"

2
A PRETTY LITTLE TOWN

NEXT morning the Cactus Boys saddled their horses and mounted up. Then they waited. After a few minutes, Snake-Eyes began to get restless. "Why don't we ride out, Red Dog?" he asked.

"Because it ain't high noon yet," said Red Dog, holding up a fat pocket-watch.

“Outlaws always ride out at high noon. Don’t you know nothin’?”

High noon came at last and the Cactus Boys set off down the dusty trail. Red Dog took out his harmonica and played an old cowboy song as they rode along.

“Hey, Red Dog?” said Snake-Eyes. “Are we gonna ride into Lavender Gulch a-hootin’ and a-hollerin’ and a-shootin’ up the town? Are we gonna dunk the preacher in the horse-trough outside the saloon?”

Red Dog put away his harmonica and looked thoughtful. "We're gonna take it nice and easy until we know the lie of the land," he said.

"But most places I've been to the land just lies down flat." Snake Eyes frowned. "Unless you come to a mountain, then it sort of stands up and – ".

"Red Dog means we have to check out the town," Dude interrupted. "We need to find out about the bank and the local sheriff."

Snake-Eyes smiled. His broken teeth looked like tombstones in a neglected graveyard. "If the bank's got one of those big, heavy safes, can I blow it up with dynamite?" he asked. "Boy, oh boy, I surely do love to hear that stuff go ka-boom!"

"This time, I'm gonna use my money to make a fresh start," Red Dog said thoughtfully. "I've always hankered after a little boat of my own so I can go fishin'... and smugglin'."

"Property, that's the thing!" sighed Dude. "I'd like to buy a trim little place somewhere respectable. Some place where my neighbours would be respectable people who'd tip their hats and say - 'Good mornin', Mr Kincaid!' Then I'd burn the house down, collect the insurance money and buy me a bigger trim little house, and burn that down, too. I reckon in a couple of years, if things worked out, I could be settin' fire to luxury hotels."

"Aw shucks!" Snake-Eyes said bashfully. "If I had me a pile of money, I'd buy myself the biggest ol' teddy bear I could find!"

"Why?" said Red Dog.

"I like teddy bears," said Snake-Eyes. "Paw wouldn't let me have one when I was a kid. He reckoned they was for cissies. That's what made me into an outlaw – I used to steal teddies from the other kids!"

It took four hours to reach Lavender Gulch and when the outlaws saw the town for the first time, they gasped with astonishment.

Lavender Gulch was neat and clean. The buildings had all been whitewashed and they glowed in the late-afternoon sun.

There were hanging baskets of flowers in every porch, lace curtains at every window and a gleaming brass door-knocker on every door. The people on the main street looked happy. Smartly dressed men bowed politely to ladies who swept along in crinoline dresses, and everyone smiled.

"Where's the mud?" said Red Dog. "Where's the flea-bitten mutt? Where's the filthy old man sittin' out on his porch, spittin' tobacco-juice into the street?"

"Where's the saloon with the drunken cowboys breakin' chairs over each others' heads?" said Snake Eyes.

"Hoo-whee!" chuckled Dude. "I guess this must be the prettiest little town I ever did see!"

"But it shouldn't be pretty!" snarled Red Dog. "It should be dirty and smelly and wild! That's why the Wild West is the Wild West! If it was all like this, they'd call it the Pretty West!"

"Howdy!" said a voice. "You're new in town, ain't you?"

The outlaws turned and saw a young woman looking at them. She wore a grey dress and she carried a matching parasol. Her face was tanned and her teeth were white when she smiled.

"Howdy, ma'am!" said Red Dog, touching the brim of his battered ten-gallon hat. "We're strangers here, all right. Is there a hotel in town? We need to get a bath and some clean clothes after our long ride."

"If you go right on down the main street, you'll come to Mrs McTree's boarding house. I reckon as how she'll take care of you," said the young woman.

"Thank you kindly, ma'am," said Red Dog.

"No trouble," said the young woman. "It's my job to help people. My name's Belle Cassidy – I'm the local sheriff."

As Sheriff Cassidy turned away the Cactus Boys boggled.

"My, my!" muttered Red Dog.

"Well, well!" whispered Dude.

"I'll be darned!" said Snake-Eyes. "The sheriff is a girlie!"

3
THE PLAN

MRS McTree's boarding house looked like a picture on a birthday card. It had a well-tended front garden and pink roses twined around the porch. When Red Dog tugged the bell-pull, chimes rang out: "There's No Place Like Home".

The front door was opened by Mrs McTree herself, a round, comfortable woman with silver hair tied back in a bun.

"Afternoon, ma'am," said Red Dog. "We were told you might have some rooms for rent."

Mrs McTree's smile was like the sun coming out from behind a storm cloud. "I've got plenty of rooms!" she said. "I've got hot baths and feather beds so soft they'll float you off to sleep. I've got steak suppers and apple pies just like your old maw used to bake!"

"My old maw never used to bake apple pies," said Snake-Eyes. "We had to eat 'em raw."

Tears welled up in Mrs McTree's eyes and she came over all motherly. "Come right along inside and let me take real good care of you!"

After bathing and changing their clothes, the Cactus Boys met on the landing before going down to the dining-room.

"I feel a humdingin', super-dooper, bank-robbery plan comin' on," Red Dog told the others. "Somethin's been jumpin' up and down in the back of my brain ever since we hit town."

"Maybe you just got your hat band too tight," Snake-Eyes said helpfully.

"Shut up, Snake Eyes!" snapped Red Dog. "And you keep your blabbermouth shut when we get downstairs! There's no tellin' who might be listenin'!"

As things turned out, Red Dog needn't have worried because there was only one other guest in the dining-room. He was an incredibly old man, so short that his chin barely cleared the edge of the table. His skin was as brown and wrinkled as a walnut shell and his eyes darted about behind the thick lenses of his spectacles like goldfish in a frozen pond.

"Howdy, strangers!" he wheezed as the outlaws entered.

"Howdy!" they replied.

"Dan Tucker's the name!" said the old man. "I'm ninety-two and I've never missed a day's work in my life! What d'you say to that, eh?"

"Incredible!" said Red Dog. "Where d'you work?"

"Over at the bank," said Dan. "I'm the guard."

Red Dog was so overcome by this news that Snake-Eyes had to help him to a chair. Dude kept Dan Tucker talking to find out all he could. "My friends and I are thinking of doing some business with the bank," he said. "Is money safe there?"

"Yup!" said Dan.

"I expect the bank vault's got a steel-bound, multi-levered, blast-proof lock on it," said Dude.

"Nope!" said Dan. "The manager, Mr Phee, keeps all the money in an old wicker laundry-basket."

Dude's eyes bulged out so far that they made a noise like balloons being rubbed together. "Th-then I guess the bank must have one of those new-fangled, automatic alarm systems!" he said.

"Nope!" said Dan. "This is such a law-abidin' town that fancy safes and alarms would just be a waste of money, son. Here in Lavender Gulch we're just plain folks!"

Over supper, Dude repeated what Dan Tucker had told him. Red Dog and Snake- Eyes were stunned.

"The sheriff's a girl, the bank guard's a crazy old galoot and the bank safe is a laundry-basket?" said Red Dog.

"Aw, heck!" Snake-Eyes frowned. "Does that mean I don't get to use any dynamite?"

Suddenly, Red Dog's eyes took on a far-away look. "I've got it!" he whispered.

"The humdingin', super-dooper bank-robbery plan?" asked Snake-Eyes.

"You betcha!" said Red Dog. "The way I've got it figured is that tomorrow we'll get up nice and early and stroll over to the bank. Then, once inside, we'll draw our guns and tell the manager to hand over the basket of money."

"I like it!" said Dude. "It's classic, direct and almost elegant in its simplicity."

"And then we ride back to the shack, right?" said Snake-Eyes.

"Wrong!" said Red Dog. "I'm finished with the shack. I ain't never goin' back there! From tomorrow, it's a life on the ocean waves for me!"

"Ah!" murmured Dude. "I can almost see that house of mine, with a cosy fire blazin' on the roof."

"And Teddy and me can ride off into the sunset!" Snake-Eyes said dreamily.

"Yes, sir!" said Red Dog. "This is gonna be the Cactus Boys' last bank robbery - so let's make it a doozie!"

4

THE LAST ROBBERY

RED's plan hit its first hitch the next morning. The gang were up well before dawn, but they didn't get to the bank early because they hadn't reckoned on Mrs McTree. She'd cooked them an enormous breakfast of ham, eggs and waffles. By the time they'd eaten their way through it all, the sun was high in the sky.

"You boys be sure to be back for lunch," Mrs McTree told them as they staggered from the table. "I'm gonna cook up a whole mess of chilli con carne that'll be hotter than a gopher on a griddle!"

Out on the boarding-house veranda, Snake-Eyes slapped his thigh and whooped for joy. "Boy, oh boy! Chilli con carne - my favourite!" he cried. "I can hardly wait!"

"We ain't comin' back for lunch, Snake-Eyes!" said Red Dog. "We're gonna rob a bank, remember?"

"Well, dagnabbit!" Snake Eyes cursed. "No chilli, no dynamite – when does a feller get to have any fun in this here gang?"

"You'll have plenty of fun countin' out crisp hundred-dollar bills," said Dude.

"I like five-cent pieces best!" said Snake-Eyes. "Can I have my share in five-cent pieces?"

"Shut up, Snake Eyes!" said Red Dog. "Here comes the sheriff!"

Sheriff Cassidy strolled towards the gang. Her dress and parasol were dark blue and her smile seemed wider and whiter than ever. "Enjoying your stay, fellers?" she asked.

"We surely are, ma'am!" said Red Dog. "We're only sorry that we can't stay longer. When we've finished our business at the bank, we'll be on our way."

A strange light came into Sheriff Cassidy's eyes when Red Dog said this, as though she knew something that he didn't. "You take real good care of yourselves," she said. "It's been a pleasure to meet you."

Red Dog, Snake-Eyes and Dude untied their horses, walked them across the street and hitched them to the rail outside the bank. Dan Tucker held the front door of the bank open for the outlaws and winked as they walked in.

Inside the bank, everything shone as though freshly polished, including the big nose of the manager, Mr Phee, who bustled over to greet the gang. "Good morning, good morning!" he said. "Welcome to Lavender Gulch Bank, where your business is our pleasure! How may I help you, gentlemen?"

"My friends and I intend to rob this bank," said Red Dog.

He reached down for his gun, but Mr Phee tutted and shook his head. "No need for that, sir," he said. "I'm sure it's all in order." He turned to speak to the two assistants who were seated behind the counter. "Carver, Mason! These gentlemen

are robbing the bank. Be so kind as to go into the back office and fetch out all the money we have."

"At once, Mr Phee!" said the assistants, promptly hopping off their stools.

"I won't keep you a moment, gentlemen," said Mr Phee.

Red Dog scratched his chin thoughtfully. "You're mighty cool for a man whose bank's bein' robbed," he said.

"Here at Lavender Gulch Bank we believe that the customer is always right," Mr Phee explained.

The assistants appeared, carrying the heavy laundry-basket between them. They set it down at the feet of the gang.

"Would you like us to help you carry it outside?" asked one of the assistants.

Snake-Eyes snatched off his hat, flung it to the floor and stamped on it. "This ain't no good!" he yelled. "Bank robbin' ought to have screamin' and cussin' and shootin'! This is just too golldurned nice!"

"Quit complainin', will you?" snapped Red Dog.

"Can we at least have ourselves a hoot and a holler as we ride out of town?" pleaded Snake-Eyes.

"Well, OK, then," Red Dog agreed. "Just for old times' sake."

The outlaws left the bank and mounted their horses. Red Dog slapped his bulging saddle-bags and yelled out.

“YAA-HOO!” shouted Dude.

“Er, hip-hip hurrah!” exclaimed Snake-Eyes.

Red Dog eyed him curiously. “What kind of a hoot and a holler was that, Snake-Eyes?” he demanded.

“Aw, shucks!” Snake-Eyes said sulkily. “After YEE-HAW and YAA-HOO, it was all I could think of!”

The Cactus Boys galloped off down the main street. The hoofs of their horses sounded like thunder and a huge cloud of dust billowed up behind them.

"Nothin' can stop us now!" cried Red Dog.

But he was wrong, because just on the outskirts of town they met a solitary figure standing in the middle of the road, blocking their way. It was Sheriff Belle Cassidy.

The Cactus Boys reined their horses to a halt. "Ma'am," said Red Dog, "the boys and me would be much obliged if you'd step aside. We don't want anybody to get hurt."

"Don't you worry none," said Sheriff Cassidy. "Nobody's goin' to get hurt. I'll see to that."

As she spoke, Sheriff Cassidy flipped her parasol into the air. Two pearl-handled six-shooters fell out of it and dropped into her waiting hands.

Before the Cactus Boys had a chance to recover from their surprise, the sheriff's guns boomed and blazed. She shot off the outlaws' gunbelts and they went tumbling into the dust.

"Th-that's the fanciest piece of shootin' I've ever seen!" gulped Red Dog as he held up his hands.

"Me too!" gasped Dude.

"Aw, heck!" said Snake-Eyes. "We've gone and got ourselves foiled by a female!"

So it was that despite Red Dog's humdingin', super-dooper plan, the Cactus Boys ended their last robbery behind the bars of the county gaol.

Red Dog and Dude spent their days smashing boulders into chips of gravel.

Snake-Eyes got a job in the prison library, where he quickly gained a reputation as the fastest rubber-stamper in the West.

During the long evenings, Red Dog and Dude talked over old times and spoke with regret about the day they rode into Lavender Gulch – but Snake-Eyes didn't join in. He had taught himself how to knit, and he was busy making himself an enormous teddy bear.